*This book is dedicated to my family and to **all** the fantastic girls I have coached over the years.*

It is also dedicated to all the girls and women who came before them who didn't let anyone else decide what kind of sports girls are "supposed to play".

Keep your stick on the ice.

Pink Laces & Pony Tails

by Rob Haswell

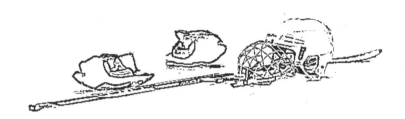

Chapter One : The Challenge

"Oh we play alright and we could beat your butts anytime!"

The words flew out of Nyla's mouth before she had the chance to stop and think. They came out of her mouth before she realized that she was challenging the top scorer on the boys travelling hockey team. They hung in the air like snowflakes while the hard cold fact that she didn't actually *have* a hockey team sunk into her brain.

"Uh oh"

Those words were in her head, where she wished her challenge had stayed. But she had to stand up to Frankie. He was so cocky and never, ever let the girls play with him and the other boys. They came down every afternoon and just took over. The girls had to get up early to practice or stay late, until the sun was almost down. It was a public rink, he had no right to be so bossy. He had no right!

"NO RIGHT AT ALL!"

Oh crud, those words were out loud too! Nyla thought.

"No right?" scoffed Frankie. "We're the league champs! Nobody cares about you and your little pink laces and pony tails. Why don't you just take figure skating like the rest of the girls?!"

"Ya step aside sieve" said Gavin the star goalie for the boys team.

He knew that would get Nyla fired up. It was the worst insult anyone could give a goalie. A sieve is that thing you use to strain spaghetti after it's cooked. It's full of holes – the one thing a goalie can't be!

"CHALLENGE"

Oh for the love of Gretzky, now I'm just blurting out words! That wasn't even a full sentence, thought Nyla.

"A challenge?! That's hysterical" laughed Frankie.

"What, like your so-called team against ours?" said Gavin.

"Ok, let's go! This should be over in two minutes!" sneered Frankie.

"Um well..." Nyla didn't have any idea what she was thinking. It was like her brain was split in two with one half shouting out crazy ideas and the other half standing back and calmly reminding her that she and her 3 friends were not exactly a match for the town's star hockey team! They barely got to practice, they'd only played for fun and they were two players short of even having a full line!

"No. Not now. In three weeks. Right before they take the rink down for the spring. If you beat us, the rink is yours.

But if you don't beat us, we get it all to ourselves, all next winter – you get enough practice over at the indoor arena anyway!"

Well, thought Nyla, at least I bought myself a little time.

"Fine." said Frankie, "It'll be fun mopping the floor with you before we go up north for Regionals. Now move so we can play."

"Oh no. We need practice time too and to make it fair we get the ice after school for an hour every other day and two hours on Saturday!"

Where this plan was coming from, Nyla had no idea but the details just kept spilling out and she was sinking deeper and deeper into the quicksand!

"Oh good grief. Fine. Practice all you want. No way a bunch of girls are gonna beat the Rink Rats." said Frankie.

"By the way," said Gavin "you need 5 skaters and a goalie to play hockey. Just because Fat Pat is 200 pounds she doesn't count as three people!" He howled at his own joke.

"OH THAT IS IT" Nyla screamed as she dropped her gloves and charged out on the ice for a fight!

Problem was, she'd forgotten to take off her skate guards and the moment her skate hit the ice she went flying backwards and landed on her butt.

The boys team erupted in laughter!

"Nice moves sieve" laughed Gavin.

"C'mon boys, we'd better let these future NHL'ers have the ice!" said Frankie.

"Is that the National Hair-bow League?" said an anonymous giggling boy in the back.

"No. It stands for Not Here Ladies" said Frankie in a voice that was almost evil. "Not now. Not ever."

The Rink Rats threw their skates over their shoulders and laughed all the way up the hill from the outdoor rink. Their voices echoed in the cold air.

The other girls rushed over to help Nyla up off the ice.

"Thanks Nyla, but you don't have to fight my battles." said Pat.

"I know. They just like to push my buttons." said Nyla.

"They're a really good team Nyla." said the girls best skater Avery.

"I know." said Nyla.

"How are we going to beat them?" asked Addie, the girls best defensive player.

"That, I don't know." sighed Nyla.

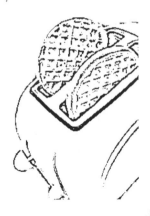

Chapter Two : Oh Brother

"Oh brother." Nyla sighed.

She was sitting at the kitchen table with her head in her hands. She'd barely touched her cereal and every time she looked down into the bowl of Cheerios all she could see was a bowl full of zeros. The same zeros she feared would be up there on the scoreboard in three weeks for her so-called hockey team.

"Oh brother." She sighed again.

This time there was an answer.

"Yes? You called?"

It was Nyla's older brother Noah.

"I wasn't talking to you." snapped Nyla.

"Well, you should be." Noah snapped back.

"Why's that?"

"Because, I heard about your little bet with Frankie. First off, what in the name of all things hockey were you thinking challenging the captain of the best team this town has ever seen?" questioned Noah.

"They're not the best team ever! They're not better than your team was when you guys went to Regionals!" Nyla blurted out. It felt a little funny saying that since she was used to fighting with her brother not complimenting him.

"Oh wow, a compliment from my little sis! Somebody call Guinness, I've got something for their World Records book!" Noah joked.

"Shut it fat head!" Ah, that felt better she said to herself, and then immediately thought she shouldn't have poked fun at her brother considering there wasn't anyone else around that knew as much about hockey as he did. At least, nobody that she'd be willing to talk about her dumb bet with.

"Hey, be nice. I can help you y'know."

"I know." Nyla said. She wanted to call him another name or tell him she didn't need his help but she knew she did.

"So what am I supposed to do?"

"Well, for starters… Catch!" Noah said as he grabbed a frozen waffle and whipped it at her. The waffle whizzed over her left shoulder and crashed into the spice rack sending the garlic powder flying!

"Hmm. You were supposed to catch that and then we'd have a nice moment where I tell you how good you are and how you can stop anything. Not sure what we do now." Noah paused. "Wanna try it again?!"

"Huh?" said Nyla.

Noah grabbed another waffle and let if fly. It sailed right past Nyla's head and crashed into the houseplant sitting on the shelf over the sink.

"Wow. This is not off to a great start!"

"Are you going to help me or not!?!" Nyla pleaded.

"Of course I am." he said.

"So what do we do first? Shooting practice? Skating practice? Trick plays? What are we going to do?" Nyla was frantic for answers.

"We are going to go spying!" said Noah.

Chapter Three : Do You See What I See?

Noah walked over to the indoor rink after school. He was supposed to meet Nyla there to do a little spying on the boys team. The idea was to try and find a weakness in the boys game that would at least give the girls a fighting chance against a team that was likely going to bring home the Regional Championship Trophy next month.

As he rounded the corner he spotted someone dressed from head to toe in black and trying to look inconspicuous in the doorway. It was Nyla.

"Oh this is not good" said Noah to himself.

"Psssst." whispered Nyla as Noah approached.

Good grief, now she's pssst'ing! Noah thought.

He turned to his sister and with a hushed but embarrassed tone said, "What on earth are you doing?!"

"You said we were spying! I'm in disguise! I want to blend in." said Nyla.

"We're at an ice rink! The only thing you blend in with is the puck! You look ridiculous!" he said.

"I'm dressed like a spy!" she said.

"You're dressed like a ninja!" Noah blurted out. "Ok, never mind, just follow me and try to look, well... normal is probably too much to ask so just try to avoid karate chopping anyone!"

The two took the back route behind the bleachers and snuck up the stairs to the observation deck that was usually reserved for coaches or scouts for the high school games, but Noah had hung around the rink for years and he knew if you jiggled the handle, the door to the room would open and it did.

They watched the practice for about twenty minutes when

Noah made a noise.

"Ahhhhhhhh"

"Ahhhhhhhh?" asked Nyla. "Did you spring a leak?"

"No. Look. What do you see." Noah pointed to Frankie as he skated in for a shot during a practice drill.

"Um. Frankie scoring at will against the best goalie in the league?" Nyla said with defeat in her voice.

"No look! Right before he shoots he drops his head, but when he passes he keeps his head up. It's a tell."

"A what?" Nyla was confused.

"A tell. It's when someone is showing you what they are going to do without knowing they are actually doing it themselves! It gives you an advantage."

"How?" Nyla was eager to learn more.

"If you know he's not going to pass you just square up for the shot. When he drops his head you know where the puck is going before he does! You can stop him!" Noah sounded excited like he'd cracked the case of the unwinnable game!

"Great, practice is over and all I have is that one little thing?" Nyla paused for a reaction but got none.

"It better be enough. Let's go." she said.

The two got ready to leave but just as they were about sneak back out of the observation area Noah stopped.

"Wait! Who's that?"

"Who?" said Nyla

A group of girls had taken the ice for figure skating practice and a short girl with bright red hair was racing around the outside edge of the rink along the boards.

"That girl going a thousand miles an hour!" Noah was excited again.

"Oh you mean Crash?" said Nyla.

Just as she said that the girl leaped in to the air with a double twist and came crashing down on the ice right on her knee. Seconds later she jumped up and was racing around the rink again.

"And that's why they call her that!" Nyla joked.

"Dude! She just landed on her knee! That's tough!" Noah's jaw dropped open.

"Ya tough luck for her." Nyla didn't get why Noah cared.

"No, that's *hockey* tough! Anyone who can take a blow to the knee like that and pop back up like it's nothing should be playing hockey! Dude! We need to get her on your team! We are switching to recruiting mode." Noah said with a flourish.

"Um ok. But you really need to stop calling me Dude!" said Nyla.

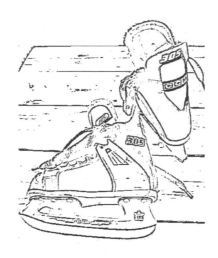

Chapter Four : Meanwhile In The Locker Room

Noah and Nyla raced down to the players benches to try and talk Crash into playing with the girls. They managed to slip by the open door to the boys locker room without being noticed.

Inside, the coach was giving the boys a pep talk.

"Great practice boys! A month from now those boys from Minnesota and Manitoba won't know what hit them!"

The boys cheered.

"Now listen up," Coach continued, "due to the tournament here next week we've got a few days off. Eat well, get some rest and keep up your off ice training! You deserve a break - just don't get hurt before we get to the championships! Now hit the showers!"

The coach left the room and Gavin walked over to Frankie with a worried look on his face.

"Hey, maybe we should postpone this game with the girls!" he said.

"Are you nuts?" Frankie laughed.

"You heard Coach! We're not supposed to risk an injury and besides we'll be a bit rusty for our game with them if we are off for a week!" Gavin was concerned.

"Wow! Did you take a puck to the head - again? We're going to the regional championships next month. We're gonna play in the same rink as a real live NHL team and you think a bunch of girls who play on a frozen puddle in the park can beat us?" Frankie was really howling now.

"Nyla's a pretty good goalie y'know. She can stop her brother, and his team went to Regionals a few years back and —"

Gavin was cut off by Frankie. He was getting mad now.

"His team went to Regionals and LOST! They're losers just like that pack of wannabe girls at the park rink and if you don't watch it you'll be joining them in Loser-Town too!"

Frankie tossed his helmet into his bag and stormed off.

Gavin stood there in shock. Nick, the Rink Rats defensive star came over and patted him on the back.

"Don't sweat it man, you know how Frankie gets sometimes. Besides, it's just a pick up game with a bunch of girls! How hard could it be? I'm not even gonna put on my good skates!" Nick giggled and walked out of the room.

"Ya. Just a bunch of girls. It'll be fine." Gavin said, trying to convince himself but it wasn't working.

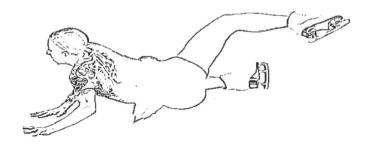

Chapter Five : Crash and Burn!

"Hey! Excuse me! Lady!"

Noah was leaning over the boards trying to get Crash to come over for a chat.

"Lady? She's my age!" said Nyla.

"Well what am I supposed to call her?" said Noah.

"Try her name." Nyla said with a smirk. "Hey CRASH!" she shouted.

"Oh nice! Great first impression." said Noah under his breath.

But, it worked. Crash heard them and skated over to the

boards. She wasn't upset, she'd gotten used to the nickname and decided it was a compliment.

"You called?" she said.

"Ya, hi, I'm uh..." Noah was nervous for some reason. Maybe it was because he had no idea what he was doing.

"Hi, I'm Noah, Nyla's brother. My Dad used to coach here and –" Nyla cut him off.

"Our Mom's a photographer, Nadia is our little sister and our dog's name is Lilly! You gonna give her the whole family tree?" she said.

"I know who you are. You went to Regionals a few years back, I used to have a crush on you!" said Crash with a smile.

"A what?" that threw Noah off a little. "Listen Crush, I mean CRASH, I wanted to know if you'd be interested in playing hockey with a girls team?" he said, happy to finally change the topic of conversation.

Crash had an odd look on her face.

"A girls team here? When did that happen?" she said.

"It hasn't and it never will" Nyla blurted out. She was getting frustrated and really starting to wish she could go back in time and take back her stupid challenge but it was too late now, there were too many people involved and too much on the line.

"Oh ok. Sure I'll play on a team that doesn't exist and after that I'll take up the fine sport of Unicorn Polo or maybe have tea with a leprechaun!" Crash said with a giggle.

"Seriously Nyla you're really not helping!" said Noah. "Listen, it's just a pick up team from the outdoor rink at the park but they're going to try and beat the Rink Rats the week after next. They're two players short and none of them are even half as fast as you!" Noah was laying it on thick now trying to make up for a bad start.

"I dunno, I could get hurt, I'm just a delicate figure skater." said Crash with a smirk.

"Hurt?! You just landed on your knee three times and –" Crash cut him off.

"I'm kidding. You had me at 'beat the Rink Rats'. Those jerks are always calling us names and disrespecting us. I'm in." she said.

"Awesome!" Noah was very relieved. "Nyla has some old hockey skates you can borrow and I'll lend you some shin pads and a helmet."

"Now I just gotta get one of those sticky type deals and I'm all set. See ya." Crash skated off with a whoosh.

"A 'sticky type deal'? Oh this is gonna be good!" said Nyla sarcastically.

Chapter Six : Start Tryin'

The bell rang and Nyla's heart sank. That was a first. Nyla liked school but in the winter the bell meant she could go out to the park and skate and shoot the puck around. So usually when the bell rang her heart jumped with joy! Suddenly though, the idea of going down to the park for a practice with the girls was scarier than a trip to the orthodontist or spending the day at bingo with Aunt Cheryl and all her crazy friends that talk too loud and have a strange smell of baloney that followed them everywhere and didn't wash out of your clothes for weeks!

"I mean, shouldn't the odor stay with the body! That's why they call body odor!" Nyla said.

"What are you talking about?" said a girl in the hallway.

Oops, I'm talking instead of thinking again. Nyla thought.

"That's how I got into this mess in the first place!" she said out loud again.

"What mess?" said the girl who was getting a little irritated by the weird conversation.

Oh crud, that was out loud again. Nyla thought. *I should really get that checked.*

"I might have a real problem." she said not noticing she was speaking again.

"Oh you've got problem alright!" the girl snapped.

You don't know the half of it lady. Nyla thought to herself being sure that she wasn't speaking out loud. Then she turned to the girl who was walking away and shouted, this time on purpose.

"HEY! Do you play hockey?!"

Nyla was desperate to fill out her team but the girl just kept walking.

Nyla took a deep breath. She was really starting to worry about the game next week but just as she was about to completely freak out and start crying she remembered something her Dad told the boys when he was a coach.

"Time to stop cryin' and start tryin' " she said out loud but only she heard it and she knew she was the one that needed to hear it the most!

Chapter Seven : Lace Up or Shut Up

The girls had a few good skates together that week and they were starting to feel like a team. Nyla was in a good mood as she rounded the corner on her way to the rink for one of their last practices before the game. Her mood didn't last long.

She looked up and in the distance she could see a group of skaters out on the ice. She felt a fireball of anger brewing in her stomach! Had the Rink Rats gone back on their word to let the girls have the rink until their game? She knew it could be the other girls arriving early for their practice but from the speed and skill, even from this distance, Nyla knew that it wasn't them. She started to walk faster and faster soon she was in a full run with her hockey bag sliding in the snow and her goalie pads bounding off her back.

Suddenly she skidded to a full stop.

It wasn't the Rink Rats. It was three older boys just playing a pick up game. The girls were sitting on the bench watching. Noah stood beside the girls, just watching the boys skate and shoot.

"He's just watching!" Nyla said out loud to herself.

I have to get this blurting thing under control, she thought but then she started to get angry. She was angry that Noah was letting these guys just take their ice time! It was bad enough that the Rink Rats took over every time they showed up and now this!

"GET OFF OUR RINK!" she blurted at full volume.

The boys didn't stop but Noah spun around with a sour look on his face.

"Shut it Sis! I asked Max, Timmy and Collin to come out today. Now get your pads on and get warmed up!"

Nyla sat down with a thump. She was confused.

"What are you talking about?" she said as she glared at Noah.

"You guys need a scrimmage before the big game right?!" he said calmly.

"But these guys are..." She stopped mid-sentenced.

It was just at that moment she recognized them. They were

all Noah's team mates from the year they went to Regionals. They were at least two years older than the oldest girl on Nyla's team and at least a foot taller.

"... they're your old team! This is insane! How can we play these guys?!"

"Well, who else are you going to play huh? That other girls team in town? Oh wait, they don't exist. The Rink Rats maybe? Oh that will work!" he said sarcastically.

"But..." Nyla protested.

"But what? Should I round up some kindergarteners for you guys? Besides, there's only three of them plus a goalie. You'll be on a permanent power play – a two man advantage!" Noah explained.

"MAN advantage?" Nyla said with a snark.

"Fine, a two GIRL advantage. Just as good." he said.

"No." Nyla said, then looked into Noah's eyes with fierce determination.

"It's better."

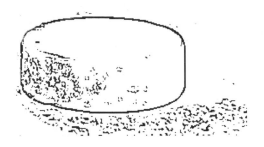

Chapter Eight : Drop the Puck - The Dress Rehearsal

Nyla finished her warm up and skated over to the girls. As she glided in she took a look at her team.

What a crew. She thought to herself. *A former figure skater, my kid sister who's half my size, three girls who've only ever played for fun, and me - the big mouth goalie!*

"I should have kept my big mouth shut!" Nyla said out loud without noticing.

"You didn't say anything yet." said Crash with a confused look on her face.

"No, not now, then. I should have shut up then." Nyla tried to explain.

"Then? When then?" said Crash.

"Big red hen!" Nadia blurted out.

The others gave an odd look.

"What? I thought we were rhyming. Aren't we rhyming?" Nadia just shrugged her shoulders.

Noah's head was whipping back and forth trying to keep up with this conversation and finally he blew his whistle to gain control.

TWEEEET!

"Shut it! Shut it now, then and the big fat hen!" he said.

"It wasn't fat, it was red!" Nadia protested.

"Ya, I'm fat" joked Pat.

"No you're not!" said Addie.

TWEET!

Noah blew his whistle again in frustration.

"Enough! Listen, if you guys can't even have a conversation without mass confusion how are you going to function as a team? Nobody expects you to beat these guys but if you can't at least give them some competition, we're in trouble."

The girls all suddenly got quiet. They knew Noah was right. Even though the other girls had nothing to do with Nyla's crazy bet, they knew the time had come to stand up for themselves and earn a spot on the ice.

The silence was broken by the other team.

"If you guys are done chatting and blowing whistles, we'd like to play!" Max, Noah's former defenseman, said and skated off.

"C'mon girls, we can do this!" said Addie.

The girls all put their hands in together forming a tiny circle. Noah looked down at the pink hockey gloves stacked up, one on the other and knew the exact right cheer to get them moving.

"Girls Rule on three... one ... two... three!"

"GIRLS RULE!" they all shouted and skated out to take their positions.

Pat and Addie would play defense. It was important to have two of the more experienced girls play on defense to try and keep the boys from scoring too many goals. Avery played center with Crash on the right wing and Nadia on her left.

Crash had practiced hard and she was super fast but still fell down a lot. Her shot was getting better and she was pretty good at passing. Nadia was a good player too but being 4 years younger than the other girls made it very hard for her to keep up. She had to take two steps to their one just to keep pace.

Nyla settled into her goal and looked down the ice. What a strange group of girls. How on Earth were they ever going to beat the Rink Rats she thought, but she didn't have much time to think before the whistle blew and the game was underway!

Chapter Nine : Wake Up Call

BUUUUZZZZZZZZZZZZZZZZZZZ!

Nyla sat straight up in bed screaming,

"NO GOAL! NO GOAL!"

She was having a bad dream about the practice game and who could blame her. The girls did their best but only managed a few shots on goal and none of them had much of a chance of going in. Meanwhile, the boys skated around them like they were orange cones and shot at Nyla over 40 times. At least 10 scored. She gave up counting after 6.

Noah appeared in her doorway.

"You ok Sis?"

"Ya. Just having flashbacks." Nyla said as she wiped the sleep from her eyes.

"Can't say I blame you. That was a bit rough." Noah said.

"What are we going to do? This is all my fault and now we're going to lose the rink because of my big mouth!" Nyla was almost crying.

Noah sat down on the edge of the bed and threw a hockey card at her. Nyla grabbed it out of the air.

"Oh sure, now your glove hand is working!" Noah giggled at his own joke.

"What's this?" Nyla said as she looked down at the card.

"It's Manon Rhéaume. The first and only woman to ever play in the NHL. She was a goalie - like you." Noah explained.

"Huh. Cool." Nyla said as she stared at Manon in her Tampa Bay Lightning jersey.

"Cool? That's it? That's not just cool, it's proof! Proof that girls can play with boys - even the best boys in the world played with her!" Noah said as he stood up to leave then he stopped and continued, "Even she had bad games but she got back in there and kept going and that's what you have to do. You started this mess and the only way out of it is for you to step up and play the game of your life on Saturday. Now get out of bed, we're going to rink before school."

Just before Noah got to the door, Nyla stopped him, "Wait!"

"What?" Noah looked back.

"Why are you doing this? Why do you even care if we win or lose this game? Why are you doing this for me?"

Nyla finally asked the question that had been on her mind for weeks. Sure, Noah was her brother and all, and they got along pretty well but he'd really only wanted her to get better in net so she could be better competition for him when they practiced together in the yard.

"It's not just for you." Noah said as he leaned up against the door. "I mean, ya, you're my sister and I'll always have your back but I'm doing this for Sammy too. You remember her?"

Nyla knew exactly who he was talking about. It was a big scandal the year that Noah's team went to Regionals. Sammy was a girl who played on Noah's team. Her Dad signed her up for hockey when she was little and just never mentioned she was a girl. She was so good that after a year or two, nobody cared if she was a girl on a boys team. No one cared until they went to Regionals and then all of a sudden everyone cared. It was a boys league, no girls allowed.

"Ya, she was the girl that didn't get to go to Regionals with you right?" said Nyla.

"Right. She played with us from kindergarten and all of a sudden it was an issue. If she wasn't so good, they probably wouldn't have cared, but a couple of the other coaches got worried about losing to a team with a girl and they demanded she get dropped from the team."

Noah paused. He looked sort of a mix of sad and mad, the way you look when you're thinking about something and wondering what might have happened if things had been different. Then he shook it off and stood up straight.

"Bottom line, she should have been there with us. Maybe she could have scored in that last game - who knows. But she should have had the chance. After that year she quit playing and that just stinks. She deserved to play and so do you guys!"

There was a long pause as Noah and Nyla thought about how important their silly little game had become.

"Now get dressed!" Noah said as he balled up Nyla's jersey and tossed it at her.

Nyla missed the throw and it hit her square in the face.

"Well that's one way to make a stop!" said Noah and he laughed all the way down the stairs.

Chapter Ten : All In

It was getting dark. The street lights would be on any minute and they would have to leave the rink for the night. Noah had taken so many shots at Nyla that her legs were starting to shake.

"I guess that's it for tonight Nyla. Good work" he said.

"No. Ten more!" Nyla said, mostly out of breath.

"You sure?"

"Yes! Just shoot and don't hold anything back!"

"Okay, I'll tell you what, you stop all ten and I will carry your bag home!"

Nyla's bag of goalie equipment almost weighed more than

she did so it was a good deal to be sure. Noah had never offered to carry it for her - ever. 'Hockey players carry their own bags' he'd always say with a smirk.

"Deal."

Noah shot hard and fast but Nyla stopped the first four. The fifth went off her helmet and sprayed snow into her face. She finally got her glove hand working and caught three in a row and the second last went off her toe and just slid wide of the net. Nyla's skates were old and a bit too small so the shot stung and she knew Noah wasn't holding back on the strength of his shots, but he was holding back. Before he had a chance to take the final shot, Nyla shouted something, but her mouth guard was still in her mouth.

"Garffle grabble bloog!"

Noah couldn't understand a word she was saying and he laughed a bit. That made Nyla even more frustrated and she spit her mouth guard out and screamed at him.

"Stop holding back!"

"I'm not! That last one just about cracked your skate open! Now just get in net! If you think I'm carrying your gear home, you're crazy!"

Uh oh. Nyla knew that look. He might have been trying to boost her confidence before but he wasn't about to get shut out by his little sister and drag her smelly gear all the way home.

Noah grabbed the puck and took off at full speed, he turned, looked up the ice and charged. Nyla got into her stance and braced herself. She knew what was he was doing. He was doing Frankie's move where he comes up the side of the ice and shoots hard for the top corner of the net at the last possible minute.

Nyla braced herself as the puck flew off Noah's stick. She lunged out with her blocker but couldn't quite get to it and a half second later a loud clang rang out across the rink.

THE POST she screamed. Maybe in her head. Maybe out loud. She wasn't sure anymore.

She looked over and the puck was spinning on its edge right at the goal line and was just about to wobble in when she reached over and sent it flying down the ice with her stick.

"The post!" Nyla screamed in delight. "You hit the post! You have to carry my gear home!"

Nyla skated over and hugged the cold red metal goal post.

"I knew you were my best friend!" she giggled.

"Alright, settle down." said Noah. "I'm a bit rusty I guess, I haven't been playing all winter like Frankie, he's not likely to hit the post."

"That's right, Pony Tail. I don't miss." said a voice in the dark.

Suddenly, Nyla wasn't giggling.

It was Frankie, he'd been watching them practice. He'd been spying on them. Of course Nyla knew they'd done the same thing at the boys practice but it still made her so mad she could spit. She wanted to yell at him but she was exhausted.

Frankie stepped into the light.

"You think working out with your has-been brother is going to save you in our little game?" Frankie laughed an evil sort of laugh.

"Watch it Frankie!" sneared Noah.

"Oh sorry, you're not a has-been, you'd have to have won something for that, you're a never-was!" Frankie snarked at him.

That was more than Nyla could take. She threw down her gloves and started to go after Frankie. Unfortunately, she'd forgotten that she spit out her mouth guard on the ice. After a couple of angry steps, her skate landed right on top of it and she fell back flat on her butt. She was too tired to even get up.

Frankie was laughing but stopped just long enough to offer a deal.

"Tell you what, since I feel bad for you, I'm willing to call off the game. Coach wants us resting up for Regionals this week anyway. Just admit you're not match for us and we can go back to reality where the boys get the rink whenever we want it and the girls pick up the scraps."

Nyla's legs were sore. Her head hurt from the stress and now her butt hurt from falling down. She felt beat already. If she took the deal at least the girls would have the ice a bit next winter.

Just as she opened her mouth to accept the deal she hear another voice in the dark. Actually it was four voices.

"NO WAY!"

It was the other girls.

Pat, Avery, Addie and Crash skated over. They'd come down for a bit of late night practice.

"Forget that deal Frankie!" Pat yelled.

"But guys, I got us into this. If I just swallow my pride, we can go back to the way things were before I opened my big mouth!"

"Oh ya, like the way things were was soooo good!" Avery said sarcastically

"Besides, these guys will never let us forget it if we chicken out now." Addie added.

"That's right, we're all in. Right girls?" Crash asked.

The girls answered with a cheer in unison, "We're in, we're in, we're ALL IN!"

Chapter Eleven : Last Practice

RRRRIIIIIINNNNNNGGGGG!

It was Nyla's new sound of dread… the school bell. She knew what was next. It was the last possible day for the girls to practice. They were meeting at the rink in 1 hour. Just enough time to get a snack, do some homework and gear up.

Practices had been going well and Noah was a good coach but he couldn't make it today because he had after school projects of his own to work on. He'd already been ignoring them for the past two and a half weeks to help Nyla and her team.

Nyla was was walking to the rink with her little sister Nadia and met up with the other girls at the corner. As they started up the hill toward the outdoor rink they noticed someone skating and shooting.

Those boys again? Nyla thought. But her gloves were pink and something looked different about her helmet.

"That's a pony tail!" Nyla blurted out loud.

"Looks like it." said Avery calmly.

"Either than or one of my Dad's hippie friends decided to take up hockey." joked Crash.

Nyla kept walking and staring and started to wonder if she knew the girl out on the ice. She started walking a bit faster and then had another one of her brain blurts.

"Holy Goalie! It's SAMMY!"

Nyla took of running, her hockey bag was bumping and twisting in the snow behind her.

"Who?" said Addie.

"Sammy? I thought it was a girl?" Pat puzzled.

"Huh, maybe he is one of your Dad's hippie friends!?" Avery asked.

"Nope. You'd smell him by now. Trust me." Crash replied.

When the rest of the girls caught up with Nyla she was

already talking with the girl on the ice and was clearly beaming with excitement.

"Girls, this is Sammy!"

"Ya we figured that when you yelled it a few minutes ago" said Crash with a smirk.

"Sammy played with Noah on his team that went to Regionals. She's awesome." Nyla chirped with glee.

"To be clear, THEY went to Regionals. I got to watch from the stands. And, as far as being awesome, well, I haven't skated in a long time. But, Noah called me out of the blue and said you needed my help." Sammy explained.

"Noah called you?" asked Nadia

"Ya. It was pretty cool to hear from him again!" Sammy said as she blushed noticeably.

Oh great, Nyla thought, this is going to get mushy and romantic all of a sudden.

"I hate mush!" she said.

Crud. Another 'out loud moment' Nyla thought to herself.

"What's that?" Sammy said, confused by Nya's outburst.

"Nothing, just... um... a random fact. I hate mush. Also not a fan of oatmeal or cream of wheat either. Just a fun fact!" Nyla said, trying to cover herself a bit.

"Ok, let's get going here. Show me what you've got!" said Sammy.

The girls hit the ice and skated hard. They wanted to show off a bit for Sammy. She wasn't really a hockey superstar or anything but around this town, she was sort of a legend.

The girls ran some plays, did some drills and took lots of shots on Nyla. Then Sammy stopped them with a loud blast of the whistle.

TWEEEEET!

"Bring it in" she said and the girls skated over.

"You guys look pretty good out there," Sammy continued "but..."

Oh great there's a "but". Just like the big ol' butt I keep falling on! Nyla thought and this time successfully kept the thought in her head.

"But you guys are trying too hard to play like boys!"

"What's that mean?" asked Crash.

"Sure, hockey is the same game for boys and girls and both can play the game well, but sometimes girls have strengths that boys don't have and boys have strengths that girls don't have." Sammy explained.

Where's she going with this? thought Nyla. Wasn't this whole thing supposed to be about proving that girls were just as good as boys?

"Aren't we supposed to be the same?" Nyla hoped that was out loud because it was supposed to be.

"You're supposed to be equal, not the same, there's a difference."

Now the girls were really confused.

"Look, at your age, most boys have stronger arms and upper bodies. If you try to out muscle them and out shoot them, you're going to lose. Your shots don't have to go 100 miles per hour, they just have to get across the goal line. Pass the puck around. Make the goalie move and get him out of position before you shoot."

"I like it." said Avery to herself.

"Plus the more you pass the puck around the more you make them skate after it and tire them out."

"Won't we get tired skating too?" asked Addie.

"Sure but remember what Wayne Gretzky said. *A good hockey player skates where the puck is. A great hockey player skates where the puck is going to be.* If you can make them play your game, you've got a real chance. Ready for some more practice?"

"Let's do it!" All the girls yelled together.

The rest of the afternoon, the girls work almost exclusively on passing. The passed it back and forth across the ice. They passed it while skating forward, while skating backward and even passed in a big circle playing a game of Monkey In

The Middle.

They only took a break from passing practice to give Nyla a few more practice shots. That didn't go well and Nyla was getting frustrated.

"Don't worry Nyla, it's just pre-game jitters." the girls assured her.

Sammy wished the girls luck and told them she'd try to come out and watch tomorrow.

TOMORROW?! Nyla just about fainted at the fact they were just one nights sleep away from the big game.

The girls all went straight home to get a good nights rest.

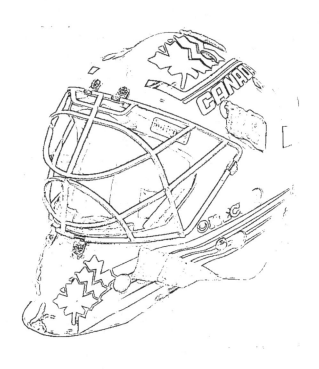

Chapter Twelve : A Dream Visitor

Nyla tossed and turned in bed. She wasn't sleeping well at all. When she finally drifted off to sleep, she had a nightmare.

She dreamt that she was a tiny goalie. Maybe the size of one of those My Little Pony dolls and the net was ten feet wide. No matter how hard she tried stop the pucks she couldn't get there in time.

She was starting to get frustrated in her dream. She started kicking the covers and trashing at her pillows but then suddenly she calmed down.

Her dream got slower and a woman skated out of fog and up to her net. At first Nyla thought it was Sammy but the dream woman was much older and had a strange accent when she spoke.

"Allo, are you de goalie Nyla dat I keep hearing about?" the dream lady said to her.

Nyla just nodded in the dream but just speaking with the lady caused her to grow a little bit and the the net shrunk too. The dream lady was talking again.

"You are very good no? You can do dis if you relax an' trust yourself."

Just as she said that another giant dream puck whizzed by Nyla and into the net. Nyla got mad in her dream and smacked the posts with her stick.

"Oh now, you shouldn't hit your bon amis - your good friends! Just relax little one."

Nyla could feel herself calming down in the dream and in real life. She stopped twisting up her sheets and started to breath a little slower. The woman kept talking.

"Ok. I know a lot about de hockey. And I see you play. You are très bon - very good. Trust yourself."

Nyla grew to full size, maybe even bigger in the dream and started stopping pucks!

"That's it! Trust your instincts and remember, a good goalie doesn't worry about de last goal, she worries about de next save!"

Nyla started to repeat that in the dream. "The next save... the next save"

RRRRIIIIIINNNNNGGGGG!

It was the alarm but Nyla wasn't panicked like she thought she would be. She was relaxed and focused. She went down for breakfast.

As she turned the corner at the bottom of the stairs she saw Noah. He whipped an Eggo waffle at her and she grabbed out of mid air then sat down and grabbed the Nutella without missing a beat.

"Nice grab. Maybe you are ready for today!" Noah said.

"I think I am." said Nyla calmly.

"Why are you so calm all of a sudden? You've been sweatin' this for three weeks!" Noah asked

"Well..." Nyla hesitated, she was worried Noah would laugh at her dream, "I think Manon Rhéaume visited me in a dream!"

"Ooo-kay." Noah wasn't sure what to say to that.

"I know it sounds crazy but I was having a nightmare and the next thing I know this crazy lady speaking half French and half English was giving me some great advice and helping me focus" Nyla paused and looked up at Noah who was trying very not to giggle.

"Hey, whatever works for you!" he managed to say between chuckles.

"Oh, whatever, at least I'm not in love with Sammy!" Nyla shot back.

"What?!" Noah protested.

"Oh please, you just called her 'out of the blue'?" Then she's all blushy and mushy.. blech! There's no romance in hockey!" Nyla yelled.

"Well maybe if they'd get more girls playing there would be!"

"Oh BARF!"

"Just be ready for the game. It starts right after school and goes until sunset! The moment the street lights come on, it's game over."

"I'm ready." Nyla said calmly.

"So, um, was she really blushing when she mentioned me?"

"Auuugh!" Nyla stomped out of the kitchen and went to rest up for the game.

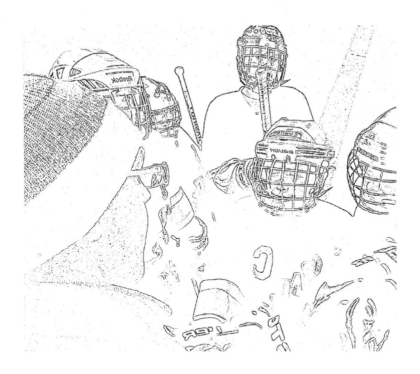

Chapter Fourteen : Game Time

Five minutes to game time. Just enough time for a few last minute words of wisdom from Coach Noah before the puck dropped on what could be the biggest game of the girls lives.

Nyla had imagined that the game day would be a bigger deal with a bunch of cheering fans in the stands, a big scoreboard and even TV commentators. But in real life, there was just a couple of kids in the stands. Sammy had kept her promise to come and other than the ref and a couple of kids riding their crazy carpet sleds down the hill, the park was empty.

Noah brought the team in for a quick talk.

"Alright, look around you. This is your team. You guys have worked hard."

Nyla looked around. Her team looked like the strangest thing anyone could imagine in their hand-me-down equipment and mis-matched sweaters.

There was Crash, the ex-figure skater who'd only learned how to stick handle and shoot in the past three weeks. Nadia, her little sister who was 4 years younger than everyone else on the team and half the size of the boys they were play. Addie and Avery, two solid defense players for sure but, like Nyla, other than playing with their brothers, they'd never played a real game. And there was Pat. She got that Fat Pat nickname back in second grade. She'd long since burned off those extra pounds but sometimes kids are cruel and nicknames can be hard to shake. She'd have to lead the attack for the girls with Nadia and Crash playing wing. Pat was fast and had great stick handling but she was no Frankie.

Nyla took a deep breath and then exhaled very slowly. She knew she needed to have the game of her life for them to win.

Noah finished his pre game pep talk and told to girls to put their hands in.

"Girls Rule on three. 1... 2... 3"

"GIRLS RULE"

Nyla skated over to the net and tapped her best friends, the goal posts lightly, she would need their help today.

The referee blew the whistle and the teams lined up for a face-off.

He dropped the puck and a mini miracle happened, Pat won the face-off!

The joy didn't last long. One of the boys defensemen quickly took the puck off her and started the charge up the ice for the boys. It seemed like seconds before the boys were charging right at the net.

Addie skated hard and managed to force Josh - the boys left winger - to the very edge of the rink up against the boards but he pushed right by her and took a shot!

It whizzed just wide of the net and Avery was able to grab it behind the net. She tried to skate it out of the girls end but Frankie was right on top of her and he snagged away and let a wrist shot fly!

Nyla just got a piece of it with her blocker and it bounced wide of the net.

This time Addie picked it up and she was off but it was all she could do just to skate the puck into the middle of the rink. Nick picked it up from there and made a quick pass up the ice to the boys right winger who snapped it over to Frankie and suddenly everything went into slow motion.

Frankie had the puck on his stick and was skating hard, right at Nyla. She braced herself and got into the right position for the shot.

Frankie leaned hard onto his stick and prepared to fire.

He's going for the top left like Noah did in practice. I just know it. Nyla thought.

But he wasn't.

In a blink the puck was slamming into the top right corner of the goal. It was moving so fast and hard that the old, frayed netting looked like it was going to barely hold. As the puck dropped to the ice, the boys cheered and skated around chest bumping and high fiving each other.

The boys had scored and it was barely five minutes into the game.

Nyla lost her temper and screamed, "SOME FRIENDS YOU ARE!"

She was screaming at her goal posts but she knew it was her fault that Frankie scored. She had tried to guess where he was going to shoot instead of waiting, watching and reacting to his shot.

"TIME OUT" Noah yelled and the Ref blew his whistle.

"Time out?! It's barely 5 mins into the game! Let's just get this over with!!" Frankie said with a sneer.

The girls skated over to Noah at the bench. Sammy was standing beside him.

"Alright, shake it off. It's just one goal. We've only got a few seconds so everyone listen to Sammy!"

"Girls, remember we have to play OUR game. You can't try to out muscle these guys or out skate them. We have to use our heads and play smart. Make them play YOUR game. Pass the puck around. For now, don't even try to skate up the ice.. Just shoot it down to the other end and make them chase it. Once they're tired, we'll make our move!" Sammy told the girls.

The Ref blew the whistle and the timeout was over.

The girls put their gloves in a circle and gave a cheer on three.

"1...2...3... OUR GAME"

As Nyla was skating back to the net all she could think about was her mistake but then she heard a whisper. It was a voice but she didn't know from where.

Man, am I thinking out load again? She thought: But she wasn't.

"Remember..." the voice whispered "a good goalie doesn't worry about de last goal, she worries about de next save!"

It was the voice from Nyla's dream and wherever it was coming from, it was right. She skated into her net, tapped the posts for good luck and whispered, "Ok mon amis... let's do this!"

The Ref dropped the puck at center ice and Pat won the face-off again. Frankie couldn't believe it happened again.

But this time Pat didn't try to skate into the boys end of the rink, she just fired the puck into the corner and let the boys chase after it.

The boys came flying out of their own end but this time they didn't get very far, the girls had set up a defensive wall with all three staying near center ice and forcing the boys to try and skate around them. Frankie made it by Nadia, stick handled past Crash but when he tried to pass it to Josh, Avery stepped intercepted it and fired it back down to the other end and the boys had to give chase again.

Once again the girls hung back and made the boys try and get past all five of them before they could get a shot on Nyla and again they didn't get very far before one of the girls was able to grab the puck and fire it back into the boys end of the ice.

The girls weren't even trying to get past center ice. They just pass the puck up until they were over the red line and shoot it down the rest of the way. They only had to get past the red line to avoid getting called for icing. When that gets called in hockey, the play stops and they have a face-off inside the the offending teams zone. That would be bad news for the girls plus they wanted to keep the boys skating and wear them out.

Over and over again they passed it around, shot it down then laid their trap for the boys. A few time they'd get past all five and get a shot but every time Nyla was ready and made the save.

The boys were getting frustrated. Frankie picked up the

puck behind his own net and just stood there while the girls waited.

"I think you can go home Gavin" he said to the boys goalie. "They're not even trying to score."

"GIVING UP YET GIRLS? CAN'T WIN IF YOU DON'T SCORE!" he shouted down the ice.

Then he was off, he passed it hard to Josh who fired it back to him at the blue line and the boys raced by all the girls defense and Frankie was ready to shoot again.

Again the world went into slow motion but this time Nyla was patient and waited for the shot. It was hard, right side again and Nyla grabbed with her glove hand and made the save!

"YA GRAB THAT WAFFLE!" Noah screamed.

"What?!" Sammy said with a smile.

"Um.. it's .. uh… inside joke." Noah replied blushing.

"You're kinda cute when you blush Coach!" Sammy said giving Noah a goofy look.

Nyla overheard that and screamed at the bench, "BAAAARRRRFFF!"

She had made the save but by trapping the puck with her glove, the face-off was in the girls end of the ice, just a few feet from the net. This wasn't good news for girls. Pat had to win this faceoff to keep the boys from a great scoring opportunity.

The puck hit the ice and Pat instantly scooped it up and pulled it back to Addie. She passed it around to Avery and she managed to get a pass off to Nadia before the boys left winger got to her and Nadia fired it down the ice. Fortunately it wasn't far enough for an icing call so the boys had to skate again and get it.

Frankie slammed his stick on the ice and shouted, "YOU'VE GOT TO BE KIDDING ME!"

He'd never lost three faceoffs in a game, let alone three in a row.

The girls were playing their game and it was working but Frankie was right about one thing, they needed to score. Without a goal, the girls might get some pride for holding the boys to one goal but they wouldn't win and they wouldn't get the rink next winter.

Time was running out. The sun was getting low in the sky and the street lights would be on soon and the game would end.

Just as Nyla had that thought the girls made a mistake. Pat had shot the puck down the full length of the ice without crossing the center red line. The play was stopped and the face-off was coming back into the girls end.

"TIME OUT!" This time it was Sammy that called it.

The girls raced over to the bench. They all had a look of doom on their faces as they looked at the sun setting.

"Listen up. It's time to make our move and Noah has a play

for you!" Sammy said calmly.

"I do?" said Noah.

"I think it's time we picked the cherries." Sammy whispered.

If this is some kind of smooshy talk again I'm going to lose it Nyla thought and managed to keep it in her head this time.

But it wasn't. In hockey they sometimes call a player who's skating way down the ice ahead of everyone waiting for a pass a cherry picker. That was the plan.

"Right!" Noah said. "Ok Pat, you've got to win the face-off for this to work. Can you do it?"

"Are you kidding me?" she asked, "I'm ownin' this guy today!"

"Great." Noah continued. "When Pat wins the draw, she'll pull it back to Addie. Addie, you have to skate faster than you've ever skated around the back of the net and up the far side boards. Crash, you need to get to the middle to get Addie's pass. But Nadia, you're the key to this whole plan!"

"Me?" Nadia said and her voice cracked a little as she instantly became very nervous.

"Yes. The moment the puck is dropped, you take off and get all the way down to the boys blue line by the time Crash gets the pass."

"But I'm the littlest kid out there!" Nadia protested.

"Exactly, they'll never expect it!" Noah said with a big smile.

"You can do this. You don't have to score, just get in there and get a shot on Gavin. Crash and Pat will be racing up behind you for the rebound. Worst case scenario, we get a face-off in *their* end for a change."

"Ok." said Nadia. She looked as white as the ice.

Nyla instantly felt awful. Her big mouth got them into this and now the whole game was resting on her poor little sisters shoulder pads! Nadia looked up at her big sister and smiled.

"We got this Sis!" she said.

The Ref blew the whistle. The time out was over. It was do or die for girls with just a few moments left in the game.

The puck dropped and Pat bested Frankie again. He was so mad he almost forgot to skate after the puck which gave Addie a few extra steps on him and she easily made it around the back of the net and up the boards.

Nadia was huffing and puffing and moving her little skates faster than she had ever moved them in her life. She was just a few feet from where she needed to be when she looked back and saw Crash get the pass. The plan was working.

But just as it looked perfect, Josh stretched out with his stick to try and poke it away from Crash. She had to jump to avoid him which wasn't a problem for a figure skater but Crash had her nickname for a reason. She made it past Josh but fell hard and sent the puck sailing down the ice. It bounced off Nadia's helmet and went flying into the corner of the boys end.

Gavin, the boys goalie, couldn't help himself and he started laughing. Who could blame him, their slick play now looked like a comedy routine. But Nadia noticed something. The Ref was waving his hands back and forth like a baseball umpire does when someone is safe at home. Nadia knew what that meant. It meant there was a no icing call! Crash didn't make it past the red line but the puck touched Nadia before going down the ice so it was still in play! She dug her skate blade into the ice hard and took off after the puck.

Gavin was still laughing when Nadia picked up the puck in the corner. He only stopped when he realized that the girls were on the attack!

You see, Crash fell a lot but that also meant she was really good at getting back up fast. She was back on her feet and racing at the net full speed.

Gavin scrambled to get into position as Nadia used every muscle in her body to pass the puck hard in front of the net. It was a perfect pass, right on Crash's stick and Crash let it fly!

Gavin practically did the splits trying to make the save but the puck sailed past him into net and the Ref blew the whistle!

The girls had done it. They had scored to tie the game!

Frankie erupted like a volcano on the ice.

"ARE YOU KIDDING ME?" He barked at the referee. "That's

icing!" But he knew it wasn't and so did the Ref.

The girls didn't have much time to celebrate. The boys were tired from having to skate after the puck all game but they were sharp enough to know that they still had a few moments left to win the game.

The Ref dropped the puck. Again Pat won the faceoff but only barely and Nick quickly scooped it up and passed it up the ice to Josh.

Suddenly the boys were moving in fast and girls had used up their last bits of energy on that last play.

Josh passed it over to Frankie and they were both racing toward the girls net. Nyla squared herself up with Frankie and got ready for his shot but just as she thought he was about to let it fly, he lifted his head!

"He lifted his head!" Nyla said out loud.

She knew what that meant. He was going to pass.

She dug her left skate in hard and got ready. Frankie made a perfect pass.

Josh got set to send the puck flying and Nyla pushed hard to get across the net and get her blocker in front of the shot.

Josh shot.

Nyla stretched out for it. She heard a big thud and then... a light came on.

OH NO! Nyla thought to herself, it's the goal light! Had Josh scored?

But then she saw it... the puck.

It was laying in the corner in a tiny pile snow that had been scraped up off the ice by the kids skates.

It wasn't the goal light. It was the street light.

The game was over.

The girls cheered and threw their gloves in the air. They couldn't believe they had tied the best boys team in town!

"What are you so happy about?" Josh said. "You didn't win!"

"The rink is ours now." said Gavin who was still stinging from being scored on by Crash.

The boys were right, the girls didn't win. They had played the game of their lives and proved they belonged on the ice and deserved respect but they hadn't won.

Suddenly, Nyla had a flashback to the moment she made her crazy bet. She could hear every word as they blurted out of her mouth, "If you beat us, the rink is yours . But if you don't beat us, we get it all to ourselves, all next winter".

"If you *don't beat us*." Nyla said to herself then she blurted it out loud. "IF YOU DON'T BEAT US!"

"What are you shouting about now? You've got to get that checked." said Frankie.

"That was the deal! If you beat us the rink is yours but if you don't, it's ours!" said Nyla who was smiling so hard it was starting to hurt.

"That's right" said Pat "I was there, and that's exactly what she said!"

"So?!" said Gavin.

"SO!" Nyla said as she skated up to the boys " we didn't beat you but that doesn't matter because YOU didn't beat US!"

The girls all screamed "THE RINK IS OURS!"

As it turned out, Nyla's bad habit of blurting out strange sentences and phrases worked to her advantage. It was a technicality but it meant the girls got the rink.

"Oh come on, that's crazy!" shouted Josh.

"No, she's right." said Frankie.

He may have been a bit arrogant and rude at times but he wasn't a cheater and he was going to live up to his deal. The boys skated off the ice slowly while the girls hugged each other and celebrated.

Frankie skated by Pat. He looked around to see if anyone was watching and then leaned in and asked her a question.

"How'd you beat me at the face-off every time"

"Simple." she replied "Don't watch the puck, watch the refs hand. It gives you a few seconds advantage."

"Huh." Frankie liked the tip. "Hey, sorry about the.. um... fat stuff."

"Don't sweat it. I'm proud of my body. It's powerful enough to keep up with you and I **am** fat but it's spelled with a PH like PHAT! Get it?"

"Got it." Frankie smiled and skated off the ice.

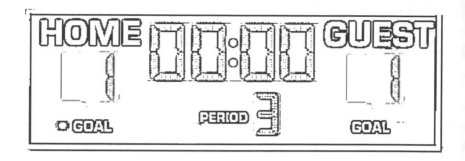

Chapter Fifteen : The Day After

Nyla treated herself to a huge bowl of Frooty Hoops for breakfast the day after the game. She was sore all over from stopping more shots than ever before but she didn't really feel anything other than pride in her game and her team.

"Nice game Sis" Noah said. Nyla just smiled back at him.

Their father came into the kitchen.

"Yes, I hear there was a big game yesterday." he said. " I hope you thanked your brother! He's quite the coach I am told!"

"Ya, he is but I think he had ulterior motives!" Nyla said teasing Noah.

"Yes, I know. Sammy called before you woke up. Better call her back Coach!" their Dad said, chiming in on the good hearted teasing.

"Oh come on now! Lay off the Coach of the year here! I

saved the day y'know. It was my play that tied the game!"

"Ya it did but you had help." said Nyla.

"True. Sammy is awesome!" Noah replied.

"Ooooh Sammy is awesome!" his Dad said as he tousled his hair. Noah just smiled.

"She was but I had another helper out there. I know it's nuts but I swear, Manon Rhéaume spoke to me on the ice and told me to focus on the next save!" said Nyla and braced for the teasing she was sure to get.

"Oh good grief! First she's in your dream then she's a ghost talking to you on the ice. Ignoring the fact that the poor woman isn't dead and therefore NOT a ghost, how do you know it was Manon?!" Noah said with a laugh.

"She's from Quebec right? French Canadian? Well she had a French accent! " Nyla shot back.

"A French accent?" her father asked.

"Ya, she said things like "mon amis" and kept calling me Little One which was odd."

"Huh" her father looked puzzled.

"What?" asked Nyla.

"Oh, I am sure it's nothing but …" he paused.

"But what?" now both Noah and Nyla were curious.

"It's just that your Great Grandmother was from Quebec.

She loved hockey. She watched every game my father and his brothers played and you didn't dare call her during Hockey Night In Canada. She knew more about that game than any man around and she wasn't shy about letting them know it. You're a lot like her Nyla."

"Huh" Now Nyla was puzzled.

"I'm sure it's just a coincidence but she would always call everyone "Little One". I think it's because she couldn't remember their names." Nyla's Dad laughed at his own joke and left the room.

Noah and Nyla sat there in silence for a long moment.

"Ok, that's weird" Noah said and got up to leave.

Nyla sat there for a while longer sipping the cereal milk at the bottom of her bowl. Maybe her Great Grandmother had come to her in a dream and whispered in her ear from beyond and maybe it was all just Nyla's imagination. Either way, it was pretty cool to know that her Great Grandmother would have been proud of her and her rag tag team of hockey players with their pink laces and pony tails.

Epilogue

That rag tag group of girls did more than just "not lose" to the boys. Their game was a turning point.

The Rink Rats went to Regionals and won. After they came back Gavin told Crash their game against the girls was a huge wake up call. The boys lost their cocky attitude and practiced hard to earn their regional title. Frankie even confessed to Pat that her face off tip helped him win the faceoff that lead to the winning goal.

They are good friends now.

Noah called up Sammy again. This time it was to get her into a tryout for an all girls Junior team in the city down the road from where they lived. She'd given up on the sport until she saw Nyla and her team playing their hearts out on that cold outdoor rink.

She made the team of course.

You see, the biggest thing that came out of that game wasn't that the girls got the outdoor rink. Word got out about the team and the indoor rink decided it was time to get girls back on the ice.

Nyla and her team have been joined by another ten girls who love to skate and play and they travel to other towns and get to play for real in a real league of their own.

Noah is busy playing for his high school team and he even helps coach Nadia's team. He's already cleared his schedule for Regionals and this time he plans to come home with a trophy!

Made in the USA
Middletown, DE
27 October 2016